Emma's Oldest Friend

Ellie Watson

Created by The Johnny Magory Co. Ltd

First published 2021 by The Johnny Magory Company Limited.

Ballynafagh, Prosperous, Naas, Co. Kildare, Ireland

Ellie Watson created this story and book following a six-week writing course during 2021 with Emma-Jane Leeson of The Johnny Magory Company Ltd.

This story is evidence that Ellie Watson is a uniquely talented and extremely capable human being with an amazing imagination and ability to continue writing books for the rest of her life.

This is an extremely special book which should be treasured for generations to come.

For my mum, dad and my two little brothers,
Sam, Oliver and Granny

Meet the characters

Emma

Emma has long blonde hair down to her waist. She always lets it down. Her eyes are bright blue and when she cries (which is not very often) her eyes look like glass. She is very tall and skinny. She loves being in creepy dark houses with mice. She wanted a mouse for her birthday, but her Mum hated mice, so she got Max. She actually sleeps with the room completely dark. She hates having to look after things that are valuable, because she is clumsy so she would break it and get in trouble. She also hates doing chores. Who doesn't? She lives on the outskirts of the village of Lockrock.

Livy

Livy has long hazelnut hair that she always ties in a ponytail. Her eyes are similar to her younger sister's eyes, except they are a lot darker. She is tall like her younger sister. She is so tall, she is taller than her mum. She likes sport and playing tricks on her younger sister. She hates doing the shopping and picking-up Max's dog poo.

Max

Max is the only one that keeps the house happy. Emma got Max as a birthday present when she was ten instead of a mouse. Max is an English springer spaniel. He has long fur and has not had a cut in a few months. He is the best dog in the world to have as a pet. Emma played with him every day outside for hours. After a month, Livy started to play with him in the mornings and then he followed Emma off into her little adventures.

Chapter 1

The big grey shape

I woke up steaming hot. The covers were stuck to me and the pillow was wet and soggy. My back was stuck to the mattress. I peeled off the covers and surprisingly, they were dripping wet. I did not feel that hot. My pillow was now a complete white slop on the bed. Every time I put my head on it, it oozed out more water!

I have an older sister who is always telling me what to do and if I do not do it, she gets revenge by pranking me. Yesterday she told me to do her laundry and I just ignored her, so she decided to drench me when I was asleep. I never wake up unless it is eight a.m. So, if you sat on me, I would still be asleep. I got up and waddled over to the door and went to my mum's room to wake her up.

"Mum, wake up I'm soaking wet!" I said, trying to jerk her awake and trying not to drip on her. If get the tiniest drop of water on her when she is sleeping, she gets ANGRY.

"Why do I have to wake up so early when your sister is outside playing with Max." mumbled Mum through her hands.

"Because she is the one who dumped a barrel of water over me!" I chattered.

"Get her or- What did you say?" asked Mum, turning around twisting all the covers, she likes to keep smooth and straight. Mum noticed the small droplets falling from her nightie.

"She did not! Do not lie about her pouring a bucket of water over you. You must have wet the bed," said Mum outraged. I was so angry with Livy that I forgot that if I said anything rude about her, Mum would get angry.

"Sorry but I am freezing cold" I shivered. There was a puddle of water all around me, so my feet were starting to wrinkle.

"Can you help me?" I asked, wanting to be in warm clothes again.

After I was in warm clothes, I was looking for something to eat. The cupboards were empty, so I had to go without breakfast. I ran out of the open door and picked Max up.

"Why'd you do that?" asked Livy who was crouching down. She stood up and dropped the ball she was holding.

"You frighten him in your little adventures so why don't you let him be and play in the sun with me?"

"Because Livy, you have your time to play with him and now it's my turn. And besides this is my dog." I said bringing him inside.

“Did you not go shopping yesterday?” I called from inside the house.

“Yes, I did. And I told you to do my laundry yesterday and you didn't. I did the shopping, you do the laundry,” said Livy, putting all the toys back in the box. The only thing she did in the work area was put all Max’s toys away.

“How come every week when you do the weekly shopping it’s gone the next day and then we have no meals, just a bit of toast.” I said coming out from my room.

“Oh, I don’t know, maybe you take it all in the middle of the night and eat it all,” said Livy shrugging.

“Well, I am going down to the forest to mine and Max’s den to hang out.” I said stalking off to the forest and letting Max down so he could run with me. Secretly I was actually going to follow the deep trail in the grass and see where it led, but first I had to go into the forest until Livy was in the house. When Livy was in the house and the door was closed, I ran up to the deep trail in the ground and followed it. The trail was fading away, so I slowed down.

"Max, sniff," I said nodding at Max. I had a suspicion that the trail led up to the big grey shape. The only reason I never actually went to the big grey shape was because Mum made Livy go with me until I turned twelve so I couldn't go anywhere near that thing. I loved to go on adventures with my trusty assistant Max. Max sniffed a trail and it led to the big grey shape. A sandy path was leading up to something shining in the sunlight. There was a trail in the sandy path. I followed it up to the door and Max slowly put one foot in front of the other over to the door. I grabbed the door knocker and knocked three times. No answer. I knocked again. No answer. I gathered all my breath and pushed the door open and stepped inside. Max made a whimper, but he reluctantly stepped inside.

The big grey shape was not just a shape but a house. The hall was so dusty and smelt like a musty closet. There were huge pictures with angry looking people in them, in old fashioned clothes. Nothing seemed to be moving in the house, but I still looked around. There were stairs so I walked over. Every step I took creaked so loudly, even when I tiptoed, so no point in trying to tiptoe. If someone was in the house, they were sure to hear it. Max was pattering so lightly he didn't make a sound. When I got to the top of the stairs, there were three doors. One had a big crack down the middle. The other two were just really dusty. I froze. I heard creaks and shuffles. The noise was coming from the door right opposite me. The doorknob was twisting and creaking.

"Max run!" I whispered as I wheeled around and climbed down the stairs as fast as I could, Max running after me. Before I could reach the door, something grabbed my upper arm. I started to kick and punch. Right now I kind of wished that Livy was here because she is super strong. After five-minutes of struggling, I lost my breath and stopped. I was sitting in a dusty chair. A face was staring at my face. This person staring at me had green eyes, a wide curvy smile and long red hair. She was wearing an apron with patches and rips everywhere. There was a trolley with a plate of crumbs and an empty cup of tea.

"Hi." She whispered, "Want something to eat?" "No! Just let me go!" I shouted, starting to struggle again.

"Stop it you will wake up the master," she whispered nervously.

"No, I won't stop until you let me go," I said through gritted teeth.

"Well, that is not going to happen, because what you have seen is to be kept secret." said the servant. I noticed something else on the tray. It was the bread we always buy and the brand of yogurt we buy. I started to breathe and calm down. It all made sense now, the disappearance of our food every time Livy goes shopping.

"So, you took it all," I mumbled.

"Speak up," said the servant.

"You took all our food," I said more loudly.

"Oh, eh," said the servant biting her nails and pushing the trolley away behind her.

"Yes, I did. The Master can't go shopping and I can't or else there would be visitors and the Master has to be kept a secret. So, instead I visit the nearest house during the night to take their food when they do the shopping," said the servant, gathering her courage to speak clearly and confess.

"Can I go now?" I asked, hoping maybe in the servant's moment of shame maybe she would be let off.

"Only if you promise to never tell anybody who lives in this house?" asked the servant.

"No way. No one appreciates what I do. When I get back, I am telling the whole village, and everybody will know," I said standing up. The servant pushed me back down and said,

"Well then you don't leave until you promise not to tell anyone."

"Where's Max?" I asked, craning my head to see if I could spot Max's long hair.

"Who?" asked the servant.

"Max. My dog." I said.

"We locked him up in the storage closet," said the servant.

"What?!" I asked.

Within a few seconds, I had broken free and was opening every door in the house. No Max. I stormed upstairs and opened the door with the crack in it. Max shot out and started to bark loudly. He jumped into my arms and started to lick my face.

"Who are you?" I asked looking at the servant who had followed me.

"Oh, my name is Daisy," said the servant.

"No. I mean, who are you to lock my dog up in a storage closet," I said fuming.

"Daisy!" said a muffled voice from the room where the noise was coming from when I first went upstairs. So now I know something lives in the big grey shape. Not only one but quite a few.

Chapter 2

Get out of the house

I was forced to stay at the house for the night. I refused and tried to escape so many times that they had to lock me in with Max. I had no choice but to sleep in the horrible grey covers and think of a way out of there. I woke up very early and Max was still asleep. Daisy, or someone, was doing something downstairs because I heard the creaking.

"Max, wake up, let's see if we can find a way out of here." I whispered. I crept over to the window and pulled the bottom up. It was open. I stuck my head out of the window and saw the ground was very low down. I knew that if I jumped, I would probably break a lot of bones in my body. I closed the window and went over to thc door and grasped the handle. I gave it a jerk, but it would not push open. I started to bang the walls which was completely pointless, but I was so desperate to get out of there, I kept on going. I heard footsteps hurrying up the stairs. Someone unlocked the door with a *click* and came into the room. Daisy, followed by two more people came inside and took hold of me and brought me downstairs.

"Max!" I screamed.

"Get out of here and get Livy!" That was a mistake because the other two grabbed Max and followed Daisy and I. Max wasn't going to be held captive, so he bit the person holding him and charged down the stairs. He started pawing the door which did not work. He ran into the living room and jumped out an open window. He charged through the grass and towards the little cottage.

The people brought me into a kitchen with barely any light. They sat me down on a hard wooden chair. They also locked the door of the kitchen just in case I was going to make a run for it. They started to pull out cups and plates and started to make something to eat.

"Stop shouting!" whispered Daisy alarmed.

"Why should I?" I said.

"Because you will wake Master up, and yesterday you made him very angry," said Daisy.

"Do you think I care whether I made him angry or not?" I said.

"No. But please be quiet!" Daisy said. Daisy loosened her grip which was a mistake and leaving the keys on the table was too. I grabbed the keys, jumped out of the chair, unlocked the door and ran for it. It took a few seconds for Daisy to realise that I had escaped and when she did, she was flying after me. I threw the keys in the air and ran towards my house. Daisy and another one of the servants ran after me but I was too fast. I saw Max and Livy running towards me. Now the servants have been seen by another person so there was very little hope for Daisy keeping life in the house a secret.

"Now we need to just get away from them and get back our house because they won't follow us into a house!" I panted to Livy when we had collided into each other, trying to stop. We were getting closer and closer to the cottage and the servants had started to slow down. We burst through the door and panted for five minutes. "Where were you?" asked Livy, punching me.

"In that house," I said, punching her back.

Chapter 3

The Man

"Emma!" screamed Mum, "Where have you been! It's been one whole day. What were you thinking?"

"Sorry I..." Before I could answer her, there was a knock on the door. I froze. They had come to our house.

"What! You said they wouldn't come to our house." said Livy.

"Well maybe they would and just not tell their location. Or maybe it's just the Master they won't talk about." I said.

No one answered the door. Another knock on the door. The next time they did not knock. Daisy kicked the door right down.

"Hey! Put that back!" screeched Mum.

"Not a chance!" said Daisy. The other two were there too.

"Who are you and where do you come from?" asked Mum.

"I am going to call the police," Mum started to rummage around to find a phone.

"You two will come with me!" said Daisy.

"Since when did you think we would listen to you?" I said.

"Never, but we have our ways," said Daisy, "Oh, look outside." I heard Max barking.

"Max!" I bellowed from inside the house. I ran out, but Livy stayed.

"It's a trick. Max will be fine," called Livy. Livy was right. The servants grabbed me and ran off with me and Max.

"Emma!" shouted Mum, "Come back!"

"How can I," I bellowed back.

"Eh... Punch kick eh... Bite, Hit eh..." screamed Mum. I really thought doing what Mum said was not going to work. But I was not going to let some weirdos who stole our food and never even talked to us, take me, so I kicked and bit and punched and hit. It really was no use because the person holding me was a man and was very strong and had a firm grip. They brought me back to the house. Mum and Livy were running after me and saw them running to the house with me, so now the whole family knew about the house. Except Dad. Now for sure Mum would call the police and tell the whole village. Maybe they would run after me. No, they stopped and ran back for the house.

Someone greeted us at the door. It was a man. This must have been the 'Master' that Daisy talked about all the time. The man had an extremely withered face. It looked very much like a banana. His eyes were grey and really dull. He was wearing shabby slippers with faded colours. He wore a dressing gown that looked pretty much like a rag. When I saw him, I jumped. "What have you done!" he croaked.

"You have shown three people my existence. I expected more from you Daisy Taylor." Daisy put her head down in shame and said, "Very sorry Master, very sorry."

"All three of you, get your cases, pack and get out of here," he croaked. All three of them went inside and climbed the stairs.

"You," he said to me, "Get in the house and meet me in the living room. Put that beast in the kitchen." He pointed at Max when he said this. "Excuse me," I said really angrily, "I will only do what you say, if you address my dog nicely." "Fine. Put the dog in the kitchen," said the man. When we were in the living room, the man asked, "What do you know?"

"Know about what?" I said as if he had asked me a question only a genius could answer.

"What do you know about me? What age I am? Why do I live here?" He questioned.

"What age are you? Why do you live here? What kind of nonsense is that," I said, really confused. "What age *are* you? And why *do* you live here?" "Well for years and years, I have been in hiding because people want to hunt me down. You see, I do something, no one knows about. I take this medicine which keeps me alive for longer than I am supposed to. I am five thousand and sixty-seven years old. I live here because this is the only place I can live. If I start taking potions, I mean medicine, in a certain place, I have to stay in that place and if I move to any place other than here, I die" he explained so casually, it seemed like he wanted that to happen.

"So, you are five thousand and sixty-five or whatever, and you can't leave the house or you will die? Just to sum that up." I said.

"Basically" he said, "Why is your dog still here? Put it in the kitchen at once."

"OK, OK," I said. After I had put Max in the kitchen and given him some food, I came back into the living room and asked him,

"Where do you get the potions? I mean, you steal all our food, and we don't have any strange ingredients, whatsoever. Unless you use butter, bread, crackers, cheese and so on."

"I go somewhere no one can go but me. I get the potions from this person who makes them," he replied. We sat there in silence for a few minutes. Max was barking like mad, so I let him out. So not only did the servants live in the house but a five thousand and sixty-seven-year-old man lived there too.

Chapter 4

Find the stuff

Again, I ended up sleeping in the musty smelling room. "I had asked the man like a hundred times to let me go, but he just said, "When I feel like it." "When I get back, Mum will be fuming at me for what has happened and Livy will be furious at me for letting Max get captured." I thought.

When I woke up Max was barking at me. I knew which room was the old man's, but I was not going to go into his room. I sat and thought for a moment. The servants were gone. That man probably had no memory unless it came to telling his story about his life. I could easily go downstairs and find a long metal pole and pick the lock to let myself out.

"Max, if you want to get out of here you will have to keep quiet, OK," I said, "Let's go." I could tell by the way he was barking a few minutes ago that he wanted to get out of here, so he kept quiet the whole time. I rummaged around for a few moments but found nothing but a dented fork.

"Sorry Max. There is no way out here." I dropped the fork back into the drawer. Max gave a whimper. Something shiny caught my eye. It was a key poking out of the edge of the wall. I picked it up. I noticed a cupboard with a padlock on it. It was really rusty. I tried the key in the padlock and it worked. I opened it and found nothing but an empty bottle. Why would someone lock an empty bottle in a cupboard?

"Find something interesting?" said a croaky voice from behind me. I jumped and turned around. The man was there.

"How did you get there without me hearing you?" I breathed.

"Oh, I have my ways and you have yours." he said cheerily.

"Now give me the key." His voice was a lot creepier and darker. I placed the key in his gnarled hands.

His long fingers closed around the key and he slipped it into his dressing gown pocket.

"You'd better be going home now." he said. He slowly walked over to the door and opened it. I stared at him open mouthed. I was wasting time to find something to pick the lock when it was open. I ran back to my house with Max trailing after me. My head was buzzing with questions. Why had he let me off so easy? Why had he locked an empty bottle in a cupboard with a padlock?

When we got back to the house Mum was sitting in an armchair thinking.

"Emma!" she shrieked, "The second time. If you ever want to leave the house, you are not to go to that thing."

Someone grabbed me and slung me over their shoulder. It was Livy. She brought me into her room. The room was filled with dirty clothes and empty food packets. She put me on the bed sitting up. She started to punch me every place she could reach without getting kicked by me.

"What are you doing?" I shrieked, "I just slept in a rag bundle, smelling of rotten fish! When I come back you decide to bruise me all over." "Yes. Do you think a small innocent dog would want to sleep in some weird house? Poor Max is shivering all over." said Livy.

"I'm sorry. I was trying to get those filthy hands-off Max. Besides, do you think I wanted to be captured a second time. There is a man who lives in that house, he fired the horrible servants and he let me off easy." I said, breathing heavily. "Who cares if he let you off easy?" Livy said. "Well Miss Nosy, if I had not been let off easy then Max would have been trapped in the house with me!" I yelled. I was so angry with Livy, I thought living in the house with the creepy old man was far better.

When dinner was ready, I sat as far away from Livy as possible. There were only four of us and Max sat on the ground, so there really was no chance of being more than one metre away from her. The window was right beside the table. The wind was howling outside so the food went stone cold in a few minutes since nobody really was eating. I went to bed as soon as dinner was finished. We had sat at the table for over an hour, so Mum told us it was bedtime. My arms were shivering as I sat on the chair, the wind brushing my face. The windows were open because it was sunny in the daytime. I was so gloomy I didn't bother closing the window. I let the wind swoop down over me like a chilli blanket.

I must have started to fall asleep because I started to have this dream. A shadow crept into my room and started to sing this song repeating the same words. The words were '*Suck it all, Take it all*'. The voice was like a whisper, like a spirit. Something yellow flew into a jar. The shadow held the jar and swooped out through the window like a ghost. I sat up in bed. The sun was shining in through the open window. It reminded me of the yellow ball that... that... thing caught in a jar. I thought of the last visit to the house and I stared at it through the open window. For some reason I felt like yesterday was the last visit I was going to make to the old man. Yesterday I felt more courageous. Today I felt like playing in the trees or reading a book in the garden. I think Max was thinking the same thing because when I went into the living room, he shied away from me.

"Hey. Don't worry, we are staying here today," I said, giving his chin a rub. Mum had her eye on me. "Are you feeling OK Emma?" she asked, coming into the room. She was obviously spying on me.

"Yeah" I said, jumping at her sudden appearance. She really was suspicious about something. As she walked through the doorway, she gave me one more quick glance. Me and Max ran out of the living room and went to the door.

"Not so fast!" said Livy putting one hand on her hip the other in front of her.

"Where do you think you're going?"

"Uh uh. Not this time. Not going there. Playing outside just like we used to," I said.

Meanwhile back at the man's house...

The man was sitting at a grime covered window. He only could see through the window.

"*Suck it all, take it all"* said the shadow. A little ball of blue light floated through the *closed window!*

"Hey Max!" I yelled to Max. "Catch!" I threw the ball and Max went and caught it. Something was wrong. Something was being sucked out of me. Suddenly I felt awful and sped back inside and left Max outside. Five seconds later there was a scratching on the door. Max was scratching the door. I opened the door.

"Shoo!" I yelled at Max. "Get away!" Livy heard. She stormed into the hall and shook me hard. I was not in the mood for this. In fact, I was never going to be in the mood for it. I punched her very hard in the stomach and she immediately stopped shaking me. She clutched her stomach and dropped to her knees. I smirked at her and stalked off. Max began to bark.

Back at the man's house.

He was still looking out the grimy window.

"*Suck it all, take it all.*" A little silver ball this time came floating through the window.

Max lost the wish to get inside and be with me and Livy. He trotted off into the forest opposite the house. Livy was fine now and she barged through the door and ran after Max. She started to shout his name. She caught up with him and picked him up. He opened his jaw and sank his teeth into her arm. Livy howled and dropped Max. He seemed happy and trotted off. Livy's arm was red and little trails of blood were trickling down and staining the grass.

Chapter 5

The shadow

Back at the man's house.

He was sitting at a desk in his bedroom. Three jars were sitting on the desk. Inside were little floating balls of light. One yellow, one blue and one silver. He opened the jar with the yellow ball. It floated into his hand and he ripped it into two. He had one empty jar and put one half in the empty jar and the other half back in its original jar. He did the same thing with the blue and silver balls. He took the jar with the three coloured balls and brought it to the window. He took the yellow ball and blew it out of the window, which was closed. It spiralled through the air. The shadow that was in my dream glided through the wall and followed the glowing ball. It held the ball in its long shadow hand. Its light was concealed inside the shadow. It was not to be seen, so every time someone came out of the house, it had to glide through the grass and it hid in the trees.

Mum was wrapping a bandage around Livy's injured arm. Through the bandage I could see very faint red dots. Mum had used a cloth to clean up all the blood.

"Now how did it happen?" asked Mum as she wrapped and wrapped a bandage around Livy's arm.

"Well." said Livy, "Emma thought it would be funny to lock Max outside. And then she punched me in the stomach. Max got fed up and stalked away. I go chased him. Then he bit me." She raised her injured arm a bit.

"Well little Miss Trouble-Maker," said Mum to me. "You are in big trouble. Things are not going your way. Go and find Max and don't come back if he is not with you".

I did not care whether I came back. When I was little, I wanted to live in the wild and eat wild berries. I would climb trees every day and play with wild rabbits. When I was six, I actually ran away to the wood opposite the house for a few hours. The wood got dark very early and I got scared. But, I didn't see the problem in going there now. I marched off through the grass. I got to the trees and the darkness swallowed.

The shadow the old man had sent, was still trying to deliver the yellow ball to the house opposite the woods. The shadow had to be very sly and good at camouflaging itself with dark shadows. The shadow leant and poured itself into a dark old tree that I was passing. It let go of the yellow ball out of its long claw like fingers. The Ball trailed silently through the air following me. I was marching so fast that the ball was soon far behind me. The shadows job was not done yet. The ball was far too slow, so the big shadow glided after the ball caught the ball and raced to catch up with me. The shadow would have won in a race with a cheetah. It's hard to believe that a shadow could go faster than a cheetah when it glided like someone on skates. It caught up with me in five seconds and let the ball go on top of me. It floated on top of my head but did not fall behind. The ball was sucked into me suddenly, I felt like exploring the house with the man.

"Bravery, Kindness and Loyalty, give it all back in one two three," the shadow whispered in its ghost like voice. The shadow blasted back to the house where the man lived and slithered under the gap under the door. Mum was walking past the window when the shadow moved to the house. The shadow was good at hiding from people outside but not from people who are inside.

"Livy, did you just see that?" called Mum. "What?" replied Livy.

"That th- eh I must be losing my marbles."

The shadow returned to the man and went *into him!* I heard nothing but the wind rustling the leaves and the chirping of the birds.

Back at the man's house

"That girl's dog is in the forest and will die someday of hunger if he stays out there too long. Give him this back." said the man holding the silver ball. The shadow took the ball and flew out the window. The shadow glided back into the forest and criss-crossed its way to the little dog with no companion. Inside the shadow was like a map. It could want to find one particular rabbit and it would find it but, in this case, it wanted to find Max. It found him in five seconds. He was wandering around nose on the ground sniffing a trail of rabbit smell. Max was going very slowly to keep the scent of the rabbit, so the silver glowing ball could go faster. The shadow let the silver ball go and it glided into Max. He suddenly realised where he was and sniffed his way back to the place he had left. The shadow drifted back to the old man's house and the man got him to take the blue ball to me. The shadow once again drifted off to the forest where I was emerging. I was now wondering why I had ended up in the forest and why Max wasn't with me. The blue ball was released and floated above my head and plunged itself into my head. I felt really happy now and started to skip. A biggish shape ran into my leg. It started barking. I recognized the bark.

"Max!" I cried, "Why are you so filthy?" While Max was in the woods, he had been rolling on the ground and covered his long fluffy hair in brown mud.

"Let's go home and give you a bath." I said and we walked home together.

Chapter 6

Nothing to do

"Hello" I said as I stepped inside.

"When were you so happy?" asked Mum, who was sitting in an armchair knitting an itchy jumper.

"What?" I asked.

"Don't forget, you're still in trouble. And we thought you would never come back." said Mum, putting her knitting down to come over to me. "Go and clean up Livy's room, but don't wake her up." said Mum warningly, as I pulled a face and walked off to the stairs. I made sure to stamp my foot hard making dust fall from underneath. “Emma!” said Mum warningly. I pushed open the door with force. Livy was sleeping in her bed sprawled all over the place. The covers were thrown aside and on the floor. I made sure to make lots of noise as I tidied up her mess. I threw the covers over her face to muffle the snoring she did every night. She started to snore louder, which I knew she was faking.

“Stop,” I said, throwing all the rubbish under the bed and went downstairs. Mum was throwing dog food and messily clothes in a basket.

“Why should I?” said Livy’s muffled voice, “I am still asleep.” I ignored her. Mum was throwing dog food into Max's bowl. Things were getting out of control. Mum was in one of her rages and Livy was treating me like her slave and I didn’t do anything wrong as far as I can remember!

Dark gloomy clouds were rolling in and making loud booming noises. Max was hiding under a chair barking at the thunder.

"What's for dinner?" I asked as my stomach gave a large rumble.

"Well, it's up to you what's for dinner," said Mum, luring Max out from under the chair to his food.

"What?" I asked. "You are going to help me peel potatoes, carrots and cut up some onions." said Mum, leading me into the kitchen and pulling out bags of carrots, potatoes and onions.

"Why?" I asked, perplexed, "You know I hate making dinner. I only like to eat dinner," I said miming eating.

"If you keep up like that you will be making the dinner not just chopping up and peeling." said Mum dangerously.

"But onions sting my eyes," I pleaded.

"Oh," said Mum. "Only you? Everyone else finds it stings to chop up onions."

"Can I wear the goggles you wear?" I asked hopefully.

"No," said Mum, smiling. "This is your punishment." I stormed off.

"The longer you leave it the longer you won't have dinner," Mum called after me, "I am going to make Livy a dinner."

"Fine by me," I muttered to myself, "I don't need food." I sat in my room and flung myself onto the bed. 'Why is everybody treating me like a little servant?' I thought to myself. The inside of me was crying with hunger.

"How am I going to survive without any dinner?" I groaned. My stomach was a bag of empty potatoes. I felt like I was as empty on feeling, as well as food. The door opened and Mum came in. "Oh, who said no dinner for me?" I hissed.

"OK, if you don't want any, I'll just tell Livy that she can have it. She was asking for more."

"I didn't say that!" I said holding my hand out to stop her. She put a bowl of cold soup on my bedside table.

"Thanks. It looks delicious," I said sarcastically. The soup was filled with onions. I hated onions. Mum walked out of the bedroom and I walked over to the small bin in my room. I dragged it to the side of my bed and started scooping out the bits of onion and put them in the bin. After that I scooped the cold soup into my mouth. The soup tasted like onions, but I didn't care. After I finished the soup I flopped on the bed. The soup tasted horrible. I clutched my stomach, curled up in a ball and fell asleep.

The moon began to rise and the clouds turned inky black. The trees were casting dark ghostly shadows across the grass.

Livy's arm healed up in a few weeks. Max was still shaking and whimpering when I even mentioned the house. Things were getting better with me and Mum. I was still not going outside even though I so wanted to go and do some more exploring of the house. I stayed inside and helped Mum with knitting (I think Mum would have preferred it if I stayed away from the knitting because my stitches were really uneven.) When Livy and I were alone, we glared at each other with cool mean eyes. When Mum wandered into the room, we would jerk our heads back down to the thing we were doing. Nothing would make me forgive Livy.

When Livy went shopping, the food did not disappear the next day. We had proper dinners and lunches. No more toast and butter for three meals a day. Besides the Livy and me thing, there were no more scrambles. I like doing the scramble but literally every time the blame is on me. Max was at bursting point. He had to walk slowly and not run. He was only let out of the house for walks and toilet. Mum took him on the walks because Max never ever dared disobey Mum. When nothing was going on, I tried to sneak out to the house opposite us. Mum must have two sets of eyes. One on the back and one on the front, because she stopped me every time. Nothing was going my way except Mum. She wasn't blaming me for everything Livy did. Livy was acting normal. She was trying to make me cry but it was really useless. Max was really fidgety. Being inside was making him nervous. He thinks we are sick. Max was not enjoying being cooped up like a parrot. The happy soul of the family was now the saddest of the family. He was not having a good day so far. In the morning at like 5 a.m. he started to bark. He was out of water. No one was paying attention. No one was bothered, so he started pawing on my door. I was so tired that I locked Max out of my room which made him mad. When he was finally allowed in, he was sitting in his bed and wouldn't let us rub his chin. We gave him food and water. He only took a few licks of his water and only a few bites of food. Adventures was part of him, and no adventures made him weird. He was not letting us play with him inside the living room where he hid under a chair and he hunted for a ball we hid for him. All he wanted to do was sit in his bed and sulk. Looking at Max made us feel really sorry for him. Mum and Livy hadn't known that Max was not himself so they thought if he was let out of the house, he would run for the forest across from them. He was now really sulky and didn't want anything to do with playing with any of them or taken for walks. I thought he was also going to run away again; I still didn't realise why he ran away in the first place.

All the days were really boring when Max and I should have been running around wild. The weather was getting worse, so even if I was allowed out, this is not the kind of weather that suits me. The only place we could adventure was the closet. The trees were rocking and swaying in the howling wind. The green hard grass turned brown as the dirt beneath rose up with water and slush. The windows were being splattered with rain and made a really distracting noise, especially when you were trying to read.

Livy's arm was completely healed by the time the weather dried up. Mum insisted that if I was to go out, that Livy came with me. Livy probably wanted to dump me and come home without me and when I returned, she would give out to me. So, the next day Livy came with me and Max to the house opposite us and then Max was happy again.

Chapter 7
Livy meets the man

I woke up with Livy staring at me, her hair tickling my face.

"Get off me!" I yelled at Livy. Livy started to laugh.

"Come on. The early bird catches the worm. If you want to go, you'll have to hurry up. The train leaves in five minutes," laughed Livy.

"Well then you just won't be going with me," I said, kind-of wishing she would leave me so I could go where I wanted.

"Well then you will have to miss the exhibition of the house," said Livy. She knew she would be able to drag me out of bed if she mentioned the house.

"Livy, don't you dare!" I warned her. Behind the lace curtain she could see that the weather had cleared up and the sky was a forget-me-not blue.

The ground had hardened up and was now easy to walk and run on. The trees were swaying slightly in the breeze. My ideal weather for running around in the forest. I hoped the forest had dried up because the only way to escape from Livy was to get her lost in there. She had no sense of direction. She would get lost if I hid behind a tree. She can only find her way if she has the instructions to get there. Every time she goes to the shop, she takes a piece of paper and Mum writes down left or right on this street or that street.

"If you wait for me, I will do what you want as long as it's in the forest." I said pointing out. I pictured a baby version of Livy wandering around in the forest saying, "Mommy" repeatedly. "Why?" Livy asked cautiously. I had to rack my brains and think of a lie.

"Because-eh-I want to pick some flowers for the house," I lied. Livy wasn't that smart, but she had some sense.

"OK," she said, approaching me slowly. The things she had sense with was like the name of sports teams and especially when it came to me acting suspicious. I stretched my clothes over my legs and pulled a jumper over my head. Livy was fidgeting with her feet. She was wearing an expression of anxiousness. She really had no idea what I was planning. I wanted to take it slowly instead. I had the strongest feeling that she was going to go and run, which meant she would drag me along and I wouldn't be able to hide.

"I want to go to the village instead," said Livy, "Remember the time I was lost for a few days in that heap of wood." I froze in my footsteps and stared at her. I saw my beautiful scheme of getting my annoying sister to leave me alone. I had two problems, one Livy was ruining my plan and the second Livy was different. Not like a caring, non-selfish person different but not Livy different.

"Are you feeling OK?" I asked, because I had a very strong feeling that Livy was trying to make me feel really bad and weird. Max was with me, but I felt he was on with Livy for not wanting to go to the house.

"Mum!" called Livy, who I thought that was back to her normal self. Livy blew it big time. Mum was always on Livy's side. If I called Mum, she thought I was confessing something. I hung my head back and waited for some boring football game. Mum came by Livy's side and said,

"If Livy says something, it's probably the right decision. Where do you want to go?" She asked me. I couldn't really tell her where I wanted to go. Why, why? I thought for a moment. I stormed upstairs and didn't go down until after dinner.

I was trying to sleep but my eyes were too focused on the lights that were shining on the ceiling. I heard shouting. I crept out of my room and saw Livy and Mum shouting at each other. This was very *very* unusual. I sat down and listened. I started to frown. I would usually think that Livy and Mum fighting was a good thing. They were arguing over me.

"I only agreed with you because I thought you would look after her. When she was young, she was in the forest for a few hours and you went off to play with your friends." I heard Mum shouting at Livy.

"Why do you think I did?" shouted Livy, "You never did anything to help her. I was trying to get her to look up to you but now I see why she didn't like your ideas." and with that, Mum stormed to her room. Livy might have caught a glance of me because she glared into my eye. We had a mental fight. It probably lasted all night. Mum was angry big time.

In the morning Mum was fuming at us. She spilled the cereal into the bowl making sure to spill it everywhere. Everything she said last night made me really mad. When we got to the door of the hall, Mum blocked the way. She had two pairs of shoes in her hand. She somehow had got a tracking device and she was holding it in one of her hands.

"I have decided on your punishment. Livy and you will spend the whole day together. I have bought these tracking systems for your shoes so I can be checking in on you from a distance. You will be sent somewhere you both do not like. The village, yes, but the library, where you will help the librarian sort out the new shipment of books," Mum said.

I hate reading. Livy did too. Livy was going to smash the tracking device when we got out the house and then she would go on a trip to see her friends. Mum was smart but not that smart. When we were outside and out of Mum's earshot Livy said, "I figure that if Mum notices that one of the tracking systems just disappears from her little toy, she is probably going to give them to us every time we go out. So, we need to go to the forest, leave them there so she thinks we are hanging out. Then when we are coming back, we can put them back on."

I saw a small flaw in her plan.

"What if we trample on them and then she sees the disappearance?" I said. We walked over to the forest and got ready to pull off the tracking system. Before we could get to the forest, I steered her in the direction of the village. I was staring around at my shoe looking for a small speck but couldn't see it.

"Livy" I said, "Mum has no chance of putting one on your friends so how would she know whether we were at the library or not?"

"Location." Livy said. The library came into view and I could see three whole stacks of big cardboard boxes filled to the brim with tattered old books. Ms. Moon, the librarian was old and mean. She would beat people up with her knobbly old cane, if you did something like fold a corner in one of the books or climb on the shelves. We were going to have to leave the tracking devices in the library. So, we did that. Ms. Moon was not happy about that. We ended up saying we would come every day and sort out the books. I left Livy to go and play with her friends while I walked to the edge of the village and developed a plan. There were three main windows Mum could see out of. The one at the side of the house, the one in the living room and the knobbly stained-glass pane in the door. I walked to the edge of the village. I ventured through the forest, bating all the low hanging tree branches out of my face. The forest seemed to go on for ever and ever. When I finally got to the house, I was pulling leaves and twigs out of my hair. I knocked on the door but then my sense came to me and I knew he wouldn't answer. I barged through the door and called him. Then I finally realized that the man had never told me his name.

“Hello Mr Person!” I called. I heard rattling in the kitchen, and I went to see what was making the peculiar sound. It sounded like barking, crying and talking all mixed up in a bundle. The man was sitting at the kitchen table doing something that seemed like a potion. (Livy was probably having a great laugh). The man didn’t see me. I screamed silently. I ran from the house and all the way back to the place where Livy and her friends always hung out. If I didn't know Livy, I would probably think she was a criminal. She spends her day playing in the grounds of the village stables pelting rocks at the horses while the stable man is not looking. The horses would neigh and Livy and her friends would run away snoring with laughter. The stable man knows what they do and is always on guard. I ran until I was out of breath and panted the words out that Livy's friends laughed at me. I would have thought if Mum made up a spooky story and said a man with a face like a banana, was muttering words under his breath, while he stirred the swirling mixture in a beaker, I would laugh. But when you see it, you get an awful fright and run away screaming. Livy was thinking something way off track to me. Livy came over to me and whispered in my ear, "Does Mum know about the tracking systems?"

"No!" I pant.

"Well then go away, the stable man will see us!" Livy said and walked away.

"OK, then I will just break the devices and go to tell Mum." I said, because I knew that would get Livy moving. Livy hesitated and said sorry to her friends about the sudden change of plans. The two of us walked away to the forest and walked in a few metres.

"This better be good," Livy said, pushing the branches away from her face.

"They won't want me in their group pelting rocks at horses and then who will I hang out with except you and you have no sense of fun."

"Well then maybe you could see what it's like with no friends. And besides if I was pelting rocks at you, what do you think? Would you like it?" I said.

"If you dragged me away to give a lecture while walking in the forest, I am ditching you." said Livy stopping in her tracks. The idea of Livy knowing how to get back to the stables without getting lost inside the forest, made me laugh to myself. We were passing our house now and no sign of Mum in any of the windows. Behind the thick branches I could see the outline of the house that we were targeting.

"Uh," moaned Livy, "Not that thing." Livy had never actually been in the house or met the man before. I was repeating in my mind, 'I need to get his name; I need to get his name.' Whenever I said 'the man' in my head, I pictured him sitting in his chair like a child, stirring soup singing a song.

Livy was slowing me down like always and was taking her time to pick every leaf from every single lowering branch. The house's shape was getting bigger and bigger. I wondered if the man was in his bed snoring and not in the kitchen stirring his weird potion.

When I budged the door open, a fresh shower of dust poured over me, making me splutter and cough. Livy was still pushing her way through the last bough of the tree, still pulling off every single leaf.

"Come on already." I said, pulling Livy by the arm, but of course she grabbed on to the nearest thickest branch to make it harder for me. If I let go, I thought Livy would make a run for it. She really did not want to go inside the dark dusty hall.

"If you come in the house, I will do your laundry for a week." I said and hoped that Livy would forget I said that after a while. She usually forgot stuff but when it came to remembering me doing her chores, she always remembered. Annoying! I ended up dragging Livy into the house which was really hard.

Mum was looking at the tracking device and knew that her daughters were always jumpy and looking for trouble. She locked up the house and went to venture into the library.

When Livy was in the door, she saw light and went over to the kitchen. By the time Livy saw the man, he was drinking from the beaker which had a sky-blue liquid swirling around with small, tiny bubbles floating in a circle on the top. The kitchen's light was so bright compared to the sunny fields and dark shady woods. We had left the door open, so the chirping of the birds was faintly heard. The man had finished guzzling down the sky-blue liquid and placed it down, with a cluck of glass meeting wood. He looked up and gave us an awkward look. Livy was trying not to laugh at the shape of his banana shaped head. "Let it out," said the man, who could see the inflation of Livy's cheeks. Livy did not need to laugh anymore so she decided to breathe out heavily. Livy was not in the mood to laugh. Her mood had changed since the man had sensed her laughter. This man was so old that anyone who just met him, would think he was so old that he would probably forgot his own name. How was I supposed to know if he forgot his name? He may seem like an old muddled up man, but he had a lot of sense. If you just met him, you would probably think he could read your mind also.

"Who is this?" said the man.

"OK, OK," I said, "What is your name?" The man thought for a few minutes. Maybe he did forget his name.

"Just call me whatever you want," the man said. I thought he forgot his name but now he is technically letting us name him. Livy was too fast. "OK, eh, Mr. Twist," said Livy. If she was looking at a banana, she would call it Mr. Yellow. She looks at something, then she takes a less obvious name and names it after the thing it looks like.

"What have you got there?" I said, pointing at the empty beaker with a splash of blue liquid.

"Nothing," said the man, "You should probably go now. I think your mum wants you." Livy and I glared at each other. Livy obviously thought it was my fault because I said to put the tracking devices in the library, and I thought it was Livy's fault for deciding to leave the chips behind.

The librarian, Ms. Moon needed glasses and there was no way that she would see the tiny chips. They were as small as a button. We had put them in the very corner of the library and they were barely visible. Mum was waiting at our house, holding two small button sized...tracking devices and her other hand on her hip. She wore an angry and disappointed look on her face. This was bad. What was going to happen next?

Chapter 8

In the middle of the night

Mum was even more cross than she had been. She thought it would be good to make us go to the library, but then she thought it best if she made us sit in a room with piles of books, needles and wool. She made us sit in that room for the whole day and she locked the window and door just in case we got any funny ideas. We made rude comments about each other under our breaths. After a few days, we ran out of words, so we combined words like: Evil bean, savage sausage and meany beany. The fights were pointless but at least we had something to do. Mum came and checked on us every hour. We had a mattress each, a pillow and a quilt. Livy would stare at me like a cat ready to pounce.

When the fifth week came of living in the living room, I began to grow tired and felt like there was no point in even trying to entertain myself. I had read all the books from cover to cover, even though I hate reading. I had used up all the wood and now my fingertips would ache when I touched them. Mum was passing in food and we ate a few spoons and then left the food to turn stone cold. After those scary weeks, I was skinny tired, sore and hungry. Mum hated seeing us so skinny, so she sat in the room when we ate and fed us like babies.

One particular night, it was cold and windy. I was not feeling good, but I was starting to feel more like myself. I was twisting and turning trying to get to sleep. Livy had drifted off after a few hours of staring at me, trying to get me to fall asleep. I stared with all my might and trying not to drift off.

I was asleep and was very uncomfortable. Bumps were all around me and my quilt felt like someone had filled it with golf balls. A gnarled hand reached in through the window and pulled me out. My head thumped as the person thrashed me against the window frame. When I woke up, I had a horrible headache. I do not remember leaving the window open. I woke up in complete and total darkness.

"Hurry up," said a croaky voice.

"Where am I?" I asked, panting and rubbing my head. I was shivering in the cold of the night and I was in my pyjamas. I could still hear the loud snoring noises of Livy snoring through the open window.

"Outside the house." said the man. "Sorry about the thing last month or was it or two months ago. I took your kindness, courage and your dog's loyalty." My mouth dropped open. When I was in the forest, I had not remembered if I had wandered in without realising, but now I know maybe my kindness and courage were gone, making my head go blank. The man hobbled in the direction of the house he lived in.

“No not in there,” I said. I was not OK with sleeping in the weird house. Even though I loved dark creepy houses and mice, if there is an old man wandering around, that is passing the limit. “We are not going there,” said the man.

“We are going up, but first we need to go to the front of my house.” I climbed through the window to grab a jacket and then followed him through the dark night.

We were standing outside the man’s creaky old house. He pressed a regular brick and it pushed into the wall. The brick scraped the other the remains of the wall and a loud rumbling sound started. The ground began to shake and for a moment, I thought an earthquake would happen. But then I thought, how could a brick in a wall, make a sudden earthquake. A parting in the grass appeared revealing a secret passage. The pathway was narrow, filled with bats and spider webs. My kind of style.

“After you.” said the man. I walked down the passageway for what felt like an hour. When we got to the end, I was shielding my eyes from the sudden brightness from the moon. A small cottage was sitting in the middle of a large clearing. The windows were filled with different coloured light. Loud crackling noises and banging was coming from the house, muffled by the latched and bolted door.

“What is that?” I was freezing with the cool breeze and the cold dungeon-like passageway. “This where I go after I have taken the potion,” he took out the beaker he was drinking from, except it was filled with a lilac potion now. “What does that do?” I asked, pointing at the beaker.

“It changes my age. If you have lived for five thousand and sixty-seven years wouldn't you want somebody to celebrate your birthday? All my family are dead, so instead of having a birthday celebration, on my birthday I have a drink of that potion that you and your sister saw me drinking. After that, I have this age changing potion that I am holding.” said the man, swirling the potion around.

"This friend of mine always makes me a potion, then we mix them, so I have a new age. And yes, this is my birthday, and as I told you, I don't have a birthday celebration, I have this disgusting drink. It just makes the day even worse."

A loud cackling sound came from one of the windows that had been flung open by an extremely long arm. The coloured lights became more flashing and brighter. The moon was hanging in the inky black sky like a big glowing ball. The house was in a direct ray of silver beams. The man walked up to the door casually and knocked. A tall bright woman was standing there with bright green eyes. She had earplugs in her ears because the banging was maximised ten times louder. I covered my ears and tried to shout over the noise, "What is that noise!?"

"You better come in," said the maid.

"Oh, and put these in. They will keep the noise level down." The maid had a really irritated expression. She probably had a beating headache all day. In fact, every day. It was a small house with broken bits of glass glittering all sorts of colours. The ground also glittered with spilled liquids and the house smelled really smoky.

"Mr Barley, he's here for you!" said the servant. Something in her voice was very familiar.

"Thank you, Katy," said the man.

"No problem, Mr Harbour," said Katy. I gasped at him. The name sounded so funny in my opinion. Maybe that's why he didn't want to tell me. If I was him and I had Mr Harbour for a name, I would be so embarrassed. He probably didn't want to make a fool of himself. The servant stared at me and gave a shiver. Her smile was curvy but disturbing and uncomfortable looking. She looked so familiar, but I could not touch where I remember seeing her.

"Oh, yeah," coughed Mr Harbour, "This is my old servant's twin sister, the sister of Daisy Conroy, and this is Katy Conroy." Bingo! That is how I recognised her face. That kidnapper Daisy. Katy was standing right in front of me, but I felt like she was going to grab me and keep me here. This identical twin was the same as her sister, green eyes, red hair and the curvy smile. But the curvy smile on this twin, was fake looking and wobbly. Her hair was really long, and her green eyes were very dull looking, like someone had turned the world dull by moving the sun further away. She had dark shadows under her eyes as if she had not slept for a very long time. I could see bits of un-brushed hair creeping its way out of the messy, knotty bun it was lazily tied into.

“Wait one minute!” called a high-pitched voice from the neighbouring room where all the light and strange noises were coming from. A man with a white lab coat came into the room. He had a pair of science goggles on. He lifted them up and wiped his eyes. His coat was covered in colourful liquids. His hands were black and wet and they glittered with liquid. His eyes gleamed with water. If I was this man and I stared at the flashing lights all day, my eyes would be burning out of their sockets. He wiped his eyes and cleared his throat.

“Oh yes, here it is,” he held out a bottle of what I thought was water, “I finished it a few minutes ago, it's a bit hot at the moment." Mr Barley handed him a huge empty bottle. Mr Harbour poured the lilac potion he was holding earlier into the huge bottle and dropped the clear potion into the bottle drop by drop. The potion in the bottle made a hissing sound and it turned black, like it was burning. When the burning stopped hissing, the potion turned thick and looked like liquorice. To my surprise he drank it even though he told me how horrible it tasted. I knew it wouldn't taste like liquorice, but I thought it might taste similar. Mr Harbour gagged and coughed.

"What does it taste like?" I asked.

"Like mouldy bread and rotten socks."

I made a face that made the adults laugh. "Yeah, not a great replacement for birthday parties and cake," I said, "I would rather have the lonely birthday parties than have that stuff." Katie left the room through yet another door. She came back a few minutes later carrying four cups, a teapot, a glass, and a jug of water.

"Tea or water?" she asked me.

"Whatever... water." I said staring at Mr Barley, who was now staring at a leaflet with potion ingredients. He was staring at it and I had a very strong feeling that he kept taking glances at me, when he thought I was not looking. Katie poured the tea in three cups and left the last cup empty, instead she poured a glass of cold water. I was sweating underneath my jumper and kept having to pull the neck of my jumper to release some of the hot air. The water glass in my sweating hand was about to fall and smash on the floor. I wanted to pour it on my head to cool me down, but I would have to get a hairdryer or something to dry me off. Then I would be hot all over again and probably need to find the nearest lake and jump in to cool off, and then repeat the cycle over again. Instead of soaking myself, I gulped it down. The cold-water chilled half of me but I was still really hot. I wanted to take off my jumper, but I also didn't want to. Mr Harbour was wearing the raggy dressing gown and wearing the slippers even though he was outside. He seemed cool and warm. There was a glowing fire and crackling in a grate in front of the door. Oh I soo wanted to get another glass of water and turn the fire into smoke. Katy asked me if I wanted another glass of water. I still thought she was a lot less happy and cheerful than her twin sister. I shyly nodded and she poured me another glass. I gulped it down in seconds and wiped my chin with the back of my hand.

"Well, we should be going, her mother," Mr Harbour was saying as he pointed at me, "Does not exactly like it when her daughter goes off without telling. The last time she slept in my place, her Mum nearly called the police when Daisy and her fellow workers came to get them back."

The walk back through the tunnel was cooling me off but the sweat did not dry off. Mum was going to end up noticing how hot and sweaty I was and she would start asking questions. Once you lie to her, she always sensed it and got you to spit it out. I would have to creep around and get new clothes and get changed without Livy hearing me. She would wake up if a mouse squeaked, so you would have to have ninja training at being quiet. And that's what I did. I was able to get changed without waking her up. I stuffed the old clothes under the sofa on which I was sleeping. The sofa was quite high, so I covered it up by using a stray blanket. Hopefully she would not decide to clean it up. I will end up throwing them in the washing machine and say I left them by accident. Maybe she wouldn't ask questions. I mean I have been living in a room for the past who knows how long, how would I know what clothes are dirty and what are clean? But all I have to worry about is not getting caught. She would blame me for sneaking out tonight when I would have happily stayed home but instead someone reached through the window and grabbed me out. I do not go exploring in the middle of the night.

Chapter 9

No

The next day was Saturday. When we were all sitting at the kitchen table (Mum finally had let us out because we were getting along), I was trying not to look at Mum. She was sitting there scooping porridge into her mouth as if the night went normal and no one had decided to go outside on an adventure. I sat there staring at the table seeing my reflection on the shiny polished wood surface. I was stirring the cold lumpy porridge round and round. Livy was the exact opposite of me. She was wolfing down the porridge. Unlike me, she was in a cheerful mood because she was going for something, she wouldn't tell me. She and her friends were probably going to pelt the horses with rocks again. When the table was cleared, I slumped back to my room. I walked into the room and felt like it was some other universe. The bed was so cold because nobody slept in it for who knows how long, and the room was tidy compared to the mess I'd usually leave it in. I sat on the bed (which was really weird) and then a few moments later Livy burst through the door. "Come on," said Livy.

"Why?" I asked, because I didn't want to leave. I felt so grumpy, but I didn't know why.

"Fine then," continued Livy, "I bet Mum really wants to know why you are not happy about being released from the room we lived in for – Whatever length, but I know where you went last night. I never fell asleep. I was pretending to so you wouldn't get us locked up for any longer. The man took you and you went with him, and you can't pretend you didn't, because I know. Anyway, if he is going to live there on his own and just get even crazier, well, I am going to go crazy as well. You were annoying enough before, but this man is crossing the limits. So today we have dropped the horses and we have made signs and are going parading!" she acted as if this was amazing.

"What do you mean by parading?" I asked her because she meant a lot of different things at once.

Maybe parading for more plain land or something like that.

“The signs.” said Livy, as if I was supposed to know what that meant.

“The signs, so what.”

“Signs,” she said counting on her fingers, “Man, you and parade.”

“So, you and your friends-”

“So, me, my friends and you,” Livy broke in.

“So, you, your friends and me, are going parading with the signs, to get people to believe that there is a man who is five thousand and sixty-seven years old, living in that house”

In my head that sounded complicated. Livy nodded.

“So, let's go!” she shouted. She took me by the shoulders and steered me out of the house towards the village.

“Do you mind?” I asked her. But she didn’t let go. I struggled out of her strong grip and went a few steps away from her. She had her eye on me just in case I decided to go and make a run for it. Livy's friends, who were throwing a Frisbee to each other, seemed amused. The first girl to see it, was sitting on the ground beside a pile of what looked like paper and sticks.

"Hello Livy!" shouted Lara, Livy's best friend. I really wanted to run away but Livy was faster than me so she could easily catch up with me. If it was me and my friends, I would be fine. All my friends moved to some other village. I don't know where, but they moved, so Max is the only person I have left. Max has been tired and lazy. He hadn't even come out of my mum's room, so we haven't seen him in some time. I lunged for the smallest banner and stared at it. I imagined it would be colourful bubble writing and *writing*, but what I saw in front of me was a small banner, *so* small, with typed words and printed on paper. What a cheat. No wonder they had it done so quickly, because Livy saw him yesterday. She must have spent ages persuading her friends and I could tell as when Livy arrived one of her friends didn't look too pleased. Livy picked up the banner that was the biggest and she tossed the rest at the other girls. All the banners technically said the same thing like,

'This shadow over there is a house!' or 'There is a man living in the shadow!' or 'This man lives there in the shadow!' or 'The shadow is not what you think it is!' Finally Livy's read, 'This is the man.'

Since Livy saw him, she knew what he looked like, she had drawn a terrible and I repeat *terrible* drawing of the man. She technically drew a wrinkly banana with a mouth, a nose and eyes. If people didn't know she was talking about the man, they would probably have thought she drew an alive banana, just for the fun of it. I really didn't want to take part but if I ran away, she would make me do something over the top. I know this because she whispered this into my ear, "If you run I will make you say, I am the one who runs away with the man." I had a choice, 1. Run away and say the thing Livy said or 2. Stay and look like one of Livy's friends. I was as tall as Lara so I kind of blended in. Livy and Amy were the tallest and Rebecca was the shortest. I tried to look natural like Livy and her friends, but you could tell I was really nervous. Livy wanted to make sure that everyone was ready and knew what they were shouting.

"OK everyone." started Livy, "Here's what I want you to do. We will walk in a line and in order you will shout what your banners say."

Great. Big whoopee. Just what I need, for everyone in the entire village staring at us. Livy was acting like this was going to a playground and starting up a game of tag with the other kids. A billion thoughts swirled through my head, Ms Moon staring at us, throwing books at our heads. But she was the least of my problems. I was thinking what Mum would think. I would be grounded for life. I imagined the whole village throwing rotten tomatoes, cabbages and apples at us. The whole world started collapsing and spinning. My head thumped. My eyes slid out of focus. I was really dizzy. I don't have the faintest idea why I was so worked up about some small parade through the village, shouting embarrassing stuff. I started to focus and thought, what if they believe us and think we are right or what if they think we are crazy and hate us for life. So many things whirled in my head for absolutely no reason. I grasped the reason why I was so worked up, what would Harbour think. Not something good. I thought of what he would say when he saw the drawing of him aka banana man. His face was a yellowish skin because Livy had visited her friend Lara to type, print and draw. Her mum was a book illustrator, so she had a laptop at home, but Livy and her friends were useless at writing stuff. Livy pulled me back to my senses by shaking me hard. I was back in focus so I could walk down the hill and into the edge of the village. I was holding my banner over my knees, so it was banging me and that one spot that it was hitting, was thumping now. The banners were all connected by two long strips of wood and one of the strips was the thing bashing into my leg. I held the banner higher to stop the banging, but not high enough for the crowd gathering around us to see what mine read. Out of the five banners, mine read, 'The shadow over there.' Unfortunately, I was the first in line. Great. Big whoopee. Just what I need. I am going to have nightmares for the rest of my life. MY LIFE WOULD BE DESTROYED AFTER THIS ONE LITTLE PARADE!!

Obviously, Livy was at the back of the line, barking orders. The banners were arranged in a kind of story. Livy was at the back because she had the hilarious picture of the banana. Hee hee hee.

At the beginning, Livy was marching like a soldier (partly because she had the best sign out of all of us, in her opinion) and after a while she started walking normally, still shouting on cue. My confidence grew, so after the hour of mumbling and tumbling, I was marching and shouting. Most people glanced at us and then went back to buying things from the stalls set up during the weekends for selling stuff.

When we finished our first march around the village, we sat on the nearest wall while Lara went and bought us water and a snack, with some money she smuggled out of the house. I am glad Livy didn't go to the shop, because being stuck with Livy is bad enough but being stuck with four of her friends is even worse. Lara came back a few minutes later with four scones and four bottles of water from the nearest stall. I gulped down the water and wolfed down the scone. Livy took one gulp of the water and it was gone, and she stuffed the whole scone into her mouth in one go. I wiped my mouth with the back of my hand. My hand was wet with some of the crumbs sticking on. I wriggled my hand, and the crumbs came tumbling down.

We continued our march and that was when people began to get fed up. By the time we were on our second march around the village, I was actually enjoying myself. People were holding bags of tomatoes, carrots, potatoes and all sorts of fruits. They were holding them in small paper bags and they had the perfect opportunity to throw them at us. One little boy laughed so hard he fell on the ground. It took me a few minutes to realise he was laughing about the banana drawing. His mom didn't like it and gave him a *watermelon* to throw at us. I mean come on! Who gives their five-year-old son a watermelon to *throw* at kids? I dodged and it must have looked funny because people started laughing. The people of the village were running out of things to do. They did the shopping, did some cooking and all that boring stuff. They needed some entertainment. A girl about eight threw banana after banana after banana at us. Then a family made up of a girl about seven, a boy about five, a mom and a dad, threw a family of oranges at us. In about five minutes we were dodging and twirling like crazy. Some parents let their babies squirt some milk from the bottles they were drinking. The babies gurgled and laughed in delight.

"Why are you doing this?" screamed Livy. She had just taken a tomato to the face. She hates tomatoes. She swallowed the juice and spluttered. I didn't ask questions like Livy, because I knew why these people were doing it! They hated Livy's idea! I abandoned my sign and ran out of the village and into the trees. I was definitely not going to Harbour's house now, so I ran into the forest and sat down on the damp forest floor. A loud barking came from nowhere and then a dog bounded through the woods and started licking my face.

"Max!" I said. I was delighted to see the dog that had been locked up in a room. It was his decision whether to go out and play or stay inside and he chose inside. Livy came running towards the forest in my direction. I sat as still as I could not wanting to talk or even look at her for the rest of my life. She dragged me into this, and she was going to drag me out of this by saying this to Mum. It will be a change for her as I always get the blame for everything, even the things she did. Maybe she won't be able to see her friends (like they like her anymore after what happened a few minutes ago), but as far as I am concerned that thing went wrong.

Chapter 10

Bricks and Hammers

I woke up with my hair sticking to my face and my hands were sticky. I heaved myself up and I felt like a heavy boulder. I looked around at my surroundings. Trees. Leaves. Moss. Birds. Mud. And a dog. Max must have slept the night with me lying on the ground, curled up in a ball. His fur was wet to the touch. I placed my hand on the wet dog. His long-wet fur stuck to my hand. I got up. My clothes were stuck to me and made me feel uncomfortable. I picked Max up as he started to whine. There was a light breeze which rustled the leaves and whipped my hair over my face so I couldn't see. There were thunder clouds rolling in and I dropped Max to the ground. He ran as fast as he could because he hated thunder. I ran through the door bashing past Mum and drowned out the loud shouts and deep drumming noises and bolted up to my room. The window was letting in a grey and dull light. The light curtains were billowing, so I threw a heavy object at the window. I had had enough. I ran across the hallway to Livy's room and smashed everything in her possession. I ran back to my room and threw myself on the bed and fell into an uncomfortable sleep.

I woke up in the middle of the night with my head beating. My head was filled with talking voices and stampeding rhinos. I saw big bright glowing balls bob up and down. I opened my curtains and saw a herd of horses, villagers with torches marching towards Harbours house. The people were carrying bags on their back full of hammers. They were obviously going to try and knock down the house. They thought it was funny what we said yesterday and now why were they suddenly believing us? At that very moment, I darted out of the house. Max came out with me and together we raced through the wild field and up towards the new parade of people. The torches were giving them some light so they could see where they were going.

Yes, I thought him weird and yes, he was really old (when I say really, I mean REALLY). But who decides to knock down an ancient house and kick an old man out of their only living house? Where else would he live, the tree or like a caveman. The lights were getting further away. There was no chance a girl and a dog could outrun a herd of adults on horses who were nearly there, and we only left. The lights bobbed over a small hill. I ran as fast as I could and reached them by the time, they had started knocking the bricks out.

I remembered what the man had said: If I leave the place, that I started drinking the potion in, I will die. Instead of knocking down the house they might as well have killed him. I couldn't remember which brick it was, but one of them opened the path to the house with Katy and Mr Barley. The brick had been hit and the pathway was revealed. The cold air pushed out and flew over the scene. The wind blew over me making me shiver. The cold wind spread just like the feeling inside me. I used a sponge and soaked up all the courage and poured it into my brain. The courage gathered up and I ran and shouted with all my might, "NOOOOOOOOOOOO!!!" The people stopped and stared at me. I suddenly felt really awkward and twiddled my fingers together. The people began to laugh. After seeing me, Max was not going to let some people laugh at me. He breathed in and barked really loud. They stopped because when he was angry, he was like a wolf. I cleared my throat and spoke, "Why are you doing this? Imagine if you were this old man and me and - a bunch of other people started knocking down your house. He has nowhere else to go."

Uh I just gave that away, I thought. People had ignored the tunnel completely and were staring at me. Half of the people nodded and understood, dropped their hammers, climbed onto their horse, grabbed their torches and galloped away. The other argued.

"Why? We are not the man and not his age so why should we do a little baby game of imagination," said a man putting a baby voice on for the 'Little baby game of imagination' part. I had had enough of this. I made myself angry by insulting myself. I marched over to the people and grabbed their hammers out of their hands, threw them into the tunnel leading to Mr Barley's house and pressed every brick I could, to push the button brick. The man had knocked it out but I found it. I expect Katy to get a nice full delivery of hammers!

"If you want to knock this house down brick by brick, fine! But that might cost you." The leading man laughed and said, "And what is that exactly?" "Bars," I said, when I say bars, I mean a cell. This mean man knew what I meant, and he silently hopped on his horse, with his torch and galloped away. I had kept a hammer behind my back and brandished it in front of the others. "Anyone care to disagree with me?" They repeated the method of the mean man and galloped away. I dropped the hammer.

"How tactless." I muttered. How would I be able to explain myself? I can't believe I said the thing about the man not being able to leave the house. I am sure they thought I meant how would he get a new house and have nowhere to go. I still muttered self insults. The night rolled on and I was still muttering to myself and I had an annoying dream of what would happen.

Chapter 11

A few years later

I woke up to a sunny day. I was hot, but bright. The sun was sizzling me like a sausage. The grass was buzzing with people. Wheelbarrows full of food were being wheeled around, while people carried bulging sacks full of... who knows what. I spun as I walked and looked at my surroundings. The place was buzzing with bubbling laughter and talking. The little boy who threw the watermelon was at least eight or nine. He was a regular little visitor for Max. A few weeks later I figured his name was Jake. He was like a mini football player and he loved jokes. The mother of this boy didn't exactly like me. I tried to avoid her if I could. Livy got a summer job as a dog walker. She would walk up and down the big field holding several leads and being dragged by a load of dogs. She hated work but loved dogs. Max always abandoned playing with Jake and joined the dogs for a little chat. Whatever they were saying they were enjoying it.

On the weekend markets, the marketers brought their gear and set up stalls and sold their stuff. Mum and I decided to make a stall and sell some homemade bread. During the week while Livy was at her job, we would bake loaf after loaf and sell it. All the hard work earned us some money. We placed our stall about ten feet away from the jam selling stall so often people would come and buy some bread and then buy some jam. I pulled an apron over my head and joined Mum at the stall.

A small, crouched man wearing a coat with a hood came over and said in a croaky voice, "One loaf of bread please."

“What type?” asked Mum pointing to the row of signs. “Baguette please.”

I smiled at the man. “Nice to see you,” I paused, pretending to forget his name, “Mr Harbour.” “Hello Emma Roberts.”

Mum handed him the long baguette in the long package.

“Got any visitors lately?”

He sighed. “Yes, unfortunately,” he said, “There is the most annoying Ms. Biggle.”

“Well at least there is me.” I said. He snorted. “Like you have time to visit.” He walked away with the baguette and he waved with the empty hand

THE END

About the Author

Ellie is eleven years old. She has two younger brothers. She loves reading books, writing stories and making things. Her favourite books are Harry Potter. She loves going on walks with her family after dinner, while playing with her brothers. Her favourite sweet is chocolate. In her spare time, she likes to crochet.

Lightning Source UK Ltd.
Milton Keynes UK
UKHW022101210521
384158UK00006B/83